COVID Isn't Fair

And I Have So Many Emotions!

Jennifer Gilpin Yacio   illustrated by Lynda Farrington Wilson

COVID Isn't Fair

All marketing and publishing rights guaranteed to and reserved by:

FUTURE HORIZONS INC.

Toll-free: 800·489·0727 | Fax: 817·277·2270

www.FHautism.com | info@FHautism.com

Text © 2020 Jennifer Gilpin Yacio

Illustrations © 2020 Lynda Farrington Wilson

ISBN: 978-1-949177-61-9

COVID-19, this darned Coronavirus, whatever you want to call it, isn't FAIR!

We've been dealing with it for months now and I'm TIRED of it!

I want to play with my friends! I want to run and jump and play tag.

1

We have been doing so well with washing our
hands and wearing masks and staying away
from people that are not in our "quarantine."

But I'm stuck inside or just
go outside with my family.

I love them but oh-my-goodness it
would be fun to see my friends.

Sometimes I get
so frustrated I
want to cry or
kick something.

And once I even snapped
at my little brother.

4

My mom says being angry is normal and she feels this way too. But we have to be aware of our feelings and not take it out on others.

Sometimes mom says we should have a "mad" session and stomp and yell at the COVID. When we are done, we laugh because that was kinda funny (but sure felt good!)

5

Sometimes I get scared. I see news about people getting sick.

I am anxious that someone I love will get sick — or maybe me!

7

Grandma says she feels
this way too. But if we
stay safe and follow the
rules, we should all be OK.

Sometimes I get depressed, and don't want to do anything but stare at the TV or play video games on my tablet.

My dad says he feels this way too. But we have to keep ourselves occupied with other activities. Next time, I can tell Mom or Dad I need a snuggle and to talk.

One day, we will be able to do fun things with friends again. For now —
Maybe I can scooter or ride bikes with my friends.

I can talk to them on the phone, or sometimes even see them on a video chat.

This is not the same as real playing, but it is nice to keep in touch. They are often feeling the same things I am!

Together we can make it through this darned coronavirus, COVID-19, whatever you want to call it.

It won't be easy, but we can do it.

The rest of the book is ALL ideas for things we can DO.

I share mine, then you share yours!

I have a BUNCH of things I can do when I am angry, sad, or scared.

Then it's your turn to tell me your ideas.

When I get mad I can:

- ☐ Do my angry dance
- ☐ Jump rope
- ☐ Hit a pillow
- ☐ Yell at the virus!

When I am scared I can:

- ❏ Look at pictures of friends or nature
- ❏ Pet our doggie
- ❏ Cozy up in a nice blanket

When I am sad I can:

- ❑ Listen to my favorite song
- ❑ Do something to help others
- ❑ Write a kind note to a friend
- ❑ Make a present for my grandma

Here is a little list of things I do for fun. On the next few pages, you can make your own list! What do you like to do?

Things I like to do for fun:

☐ Write in my journal
☐ Jump rope
☐ Paint a picture
☐ Garden with my family

Projects and things I can learn:

☐ Learn to use some kid-friendly tools
☐ Help with home improvement projects
☐ Start with a few words of a new language. Hola! Bonjour!
☐ Learn a few cooking skills

My name is _____

Here are some things I like to do for fun:

_____

_____

_____

_____

_____

_____

_____

_____

Here are some fun projects I would like to start someday, or things I would like to learn:

_____

_____

_____

_____

_____

_____

_____

_____

_____

_____

When I am angry, I like to:

_____

_____

_____

_____

Here are some other things I can try:

_____

_____

_____

_____

When I am scared or anxious, I like to:

_____

_____

_____

_____

Here are some other things I can try:

_____

_____

_____

_____

When I am sad, I like to:

_____

_____

_____

_____

Here are some other things I can try:

_____

_____

_____

_____

Creator Bios

Jennifer Gilpin Yacio is the president of Future Horizons, Inc. and Sensory World. Ever since her little brother was diagnosed with autism in 1982, she has been interested in autism as well as how people are affected by their senses. With an extensive career in both the publishing and autism fields, Jennifer is happy to be writing her second children's book.

Lynda Farrington Wilson has 25 years of experience that spans both copywriting and design, a tenured marketing vice president. She is thrilled to now spend her days in the world of color, texture, and pure whimsy in living her lifelong passion of writing and illustration. In her advocacy for children with special needs, Lynda has authored/illustrated *Squirmy Wormy*, *How I Learned to Help Myself*, and *Autistic! How Silly is That?*

Her Giddy Granny series *Butterfly Charlie* and *Chugga-Connor-Choo-Choo* are zany, heart-warming adventures modeled after her adorable, spirited grandchildren. Lynda has illustrated over 70 children's books in her studio, The Lime Crab Cottage, located at the beautiful Smith Mountain Lake in Virginia. Her favorite color is lime green, she loves to draw crabs, and well, she will squeeze in a bubble or two into every illustration she can, just because they make her smile.

www.lyndafarringtonwilson.com

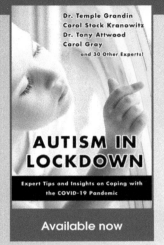

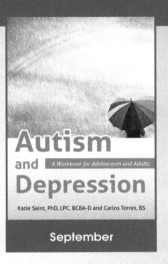

CPSIA information can be obtained
at www.ICGtesting.com
Printed in the USA
JSHW040843020920
7572JS00003B/13